For SATB Choir With Piano Accompaniment

Arranged by Chris Norton & Leroy Johnson

Cover design by Miranda Harvey
Printed in the United Kingdom by Caligraving Limited, Thetford, Norfolk

Novello Publishing Limited
14-15 Berners Street, London W1T 3LJ

O Happy Day

Traditional

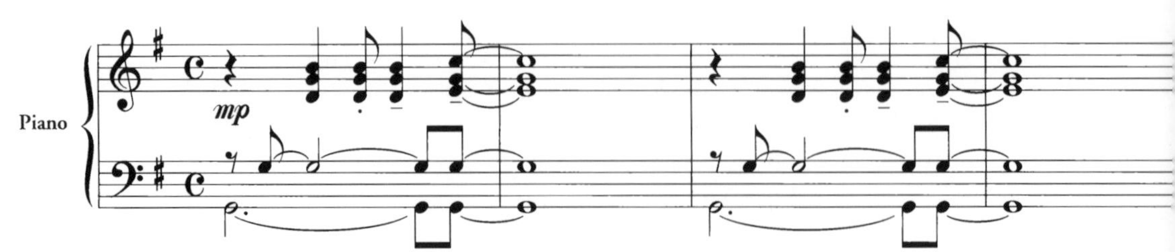

13
when Je - sus washed,

16
Ooh, when He washed,
He washed my sins a - way.

19
Mm hm, it was a hap - py day.

22

mf

O hap - py day,

O hap - py day

mf

O hap - py day,

mf

O hap - py day,

mf

O hap - py day,

mf

O hap - py day,

mf

25

when Je - sus washed.

O hap - py day,

when Je - sus washed,

O hap - py day,

when Je - sus washed,

O hap - py day,

when Je - sus washed,

O hap - py day,

when Je - sus washed,

28
Oh, ho, when He washed
when Je-sus washed,
when Je-sus washed,
when Je-sus washed,
when Je-sus washed,
when Je-sus washed,
31
He washed my sins a - way.
when Je - sus washed
when Je - sus washed
when Je - sus washed
when Je - sus washed

33
Oh, it was a hap - py day.
O hap - py day, O hap - py day.
O hap - py day, O hap - py day.
O hap - py day, O hap - py day.
O hap - py day, O hap - py day.
36
f
He taught me He taught me how
He taught me how to
He taught me how to
He taught me how to
He taught me how to

39
how to watch
watch and pray yeah
watch, watch and pray,
watch, watch and pray,
watch, watch and pray,
watch, watch and pray,
42
and He taught me how to live
watch and pray and live re -
watch and pray and live re -
watch and pray and live re -
watch and pray and live re -

45
taught me how to live re - joi -
- joi - - - - - cing e - - - - -
- joi - - - - - cing e - - - - -
- joi - - - - - cing e - - - - -
- joi - - - - - cing e - - - - -
48
- cing ev - ery day ev - ery day
- ev - ery day ev - ery day
- ev - ery day ev - ery day
- ev - ery day ev - ery day
- ev - ery day ev - ery day

51
mf
uh huh oh ho, O hap - py day
O hap - py day,
54
O hap - py day,
when Jes - sus washed
O hap - py day,

57
when Je - sus washed,
when Je - sus washed,
when Je - sus washed,
when Je - sus washed,
when Je - sus washed,
59
oh, when Je - sus
when Je - sus washed
when Je - sus washed
when Je - sus washed
when Je - sus washed

61
washed
He washed my sins a - way
when Je - sus washed
when Je - sus washed
when Je - sus washed
when Je - sus washed
63
mp
uh oh it was a hap - py day.
O hap - py day,
O hap - py day -
O hap - py day,
O hap - py day -
O hap - py day,
O hap - py day -
O hap - py day,
O hap - py day -

66
It was a
p
O hap - py day,
p
O hap - py day,
p
O hap - py day,
p
O hap - py day,
p
69
hap - py day,
oh,
it was a
hap - py day.
cresc.
O hap - py day,
O hap - py day,
cresc.
O hap - py day,
O hap - py day,
cresc.
O hap - py day,
O hap - py day,
cresc.
O hap - py day,
O hap - py day,
cresc.

72
cresc.
mf
Uh huh
oh, it was a
O hap - py day,
75
hap - py day
Je - sus washed my sins a - way,
f
O hap - py day,
O hap - py day,

78
mf
I said it was a hap - py day
O hap - py day,
O hap - py day,
O hap - py day,
O hap - py day,
80
f
ff
oh oh it was a hap - py day.
O hap - py day.
O hap - py day.
O hap - py day.
O hap - py day.

I Surrender All

Words by Judson W. De Venter
Music by Winfield Weeden
Arranged by Chris Norton & Leroy Johnson

Steadily ♩ = 63
Piano
mp

Soprano solo espress.
mp
All to Je - sus I sur-ren - der, all to Him I free - ly give.

I will ev - er love and trust Him, in His pres - ence dai - ly live.

13
f
I sur-ren - der all. I sur-ren - der all.
I sur-ren - der all. I sur-ren - der all.
17
mp
All to Thee, my bles - sed Sa - viour, I sur-ren - der all.

All to Je - sus I sur-ren - der, hum - bly at His
Ooh.
feet I bow. World - ly plea - sures all for - sa - ken,

27
take me, Je - sus, take me now.
I sur-ren - der
Ooh.
I sur-ren - der
Ooh.
I sur-ren - der
Ooh.
I sur-ren - der
Ooh.
I sur-ren - der
30
all. I sur-ren - der all.
All to Thee, my
all. I sur-ren - der all.
All to Thee, my
all. I sur-ren - der all.
All to Thee, my
all. I sur-ren - der all.
All to Thee, my
all. I sur-ren - der all.
All to Thee, my

34
f
bles - sed Sa - viour, I sur-ren - der all. I sur-ren - der
bles - sed Sa - viour, I sur-ren - der all. I sur-ren - der
bles - sed Sa - viour, I sur-ren - der all. I sur-ren - der
bles - sed Sa - viour, I sur-ren - der all. I sur-ren - der
bles - sed Sa - viour, I sur-ren - der all. I sur-ren - der
38
mp
all. I sur-ren - der all. All to Thee, my
all. I sur-ren - der all. All to Thee, my
all. I sur-ren - der all. All to Thee, my
all. I sur-ren - der all. All to Thee, my
all. I sur-ren - der all. All to Thee, my

42
bles - sed Sa - viour, I sur-ren - der all.
bles - sed Sa - viour, I sur-ren - der all.
bles - sed Sa - viour, I sur-ren - der all.
bles - sed Sa - viour, I sur-ren - der all.
bles - sed Sa - viour, I sur-ren - der all.
45
dim.
rit. . . . .
p
I sur-ren - der all. I sur-ren - der all.
I sur-ren - der all. I sur-ren - der all.
I sur-ren - der all. I sur-ren - der all.
I sur-ren - der all. I sur-ren - der all.
I sur-ren - der all. I sur-ren - der all.

Swing Low, Sweet Chariot

Traditional
Arranged by Chris Norton & Leroy Johnson

7

coming for to carry me home. Swing_ low, sweet

coming for to carry me home. Swing_ low, sweet

coming for to carry me home. Swing low, sweet

coming for to carry me home. Swing low, sweet

10

cha - ri - ot,_ coming for to carry me home. *mf* Swing

cha - ri - ot,_ coming for to carry me home. *mf* Swing

cha - ri - ot, coming for to carry me home. *mf* Swing

cha - ri - ot, coming for to carry me home. *mf* Swing

sim. *mf*

13
low, sweet cha ri - ot,
low, sweet cha ri - ot,
low, sweet cha ri - ot,
low, sweet cha ri - ot,
sim.
15
com-ing for to car-ry me home. Swing low, sweet
com-ing for to car-ry me home. Swing low, sweet
com-ing for to car-ry me home. Swing low, sweet
com-ing for to car-ry me home. Swing low, sweet

18

Tenor solo

mf

Well I

cha - ri - ot, com-ing for to car - ry me home.

cha ri - ot, com-ing for to car - ry me home.

cha - ri - ot, com-ing for to car - ry me home.

cha - ri - ot, com-ing for to car - ry me home.

sim.

21

looked ov-er Jor - dan and what did I see?

mp

Ooh. Com - ing for to car -ry me

mp

Ooh. Com - ing for to car -ry me

mp

Ooh. Com - ing for to car -ry me

mp

Ooh. Com - ing for to car -ry me

mp

24
I saw a band of an - gels com-ing af - ter me.
mp
home. Ooh.
mp
home. Ooh.
mp
home. Ooh.
mp
home. Ooh.
27
mf
Com-ing for to car - ry me home. Swing low, sweet
mf
Com-ing for to car - ry me home. Swing low, sweet
mf
Com-ing for to car - ry me home. Swing low, sweet
mf
Com-ing for to car - ry me home. Swing low, sweet
mf

30

cha ri - ot, coming for to car - ry me home. Swing

cha ri - ot, coming for to car - ry me home. Swing

cha - ri - ot, coming for to car - ry me home. Swing

cha - ri - ot, coming for to car - ry me home. Swing

sim.

33

low, sweet cha ri - ot, com-ing for to car - ry me

low, sweet cha ri - ot, com-ing for to car - ry me

low, sweet cha - ri - ot, com-ing for to car - ry me

low, sweet cha - ri - ot, com-ing for to car - ry me

sim.

36
Tenor solo
mp
Well if you get there before I do,
home.
Ooh.
Com-ing for to car-ry me
mp
40
Tell all my friends I'm com-ing soon.
mf

43

f

low sweet

f

Com-ing for to car - ry me home. Swing low, sweet

f

Com-ing for to car - ry me home. Swing low, sweet

f

Com-ing for to car - ry me home. Swing low, sweet

f

Com-ing for to car - ry me home. Swing low, sweet

f

46

cha - ri - ot com-ing for car-ry me home swing low

cha - ri - ot, com-ing for to car-ry me home. Swing

cha ri - ot, com-ing for to car-ry me home. Swing

cha - ri - ot, com-ing for to car-ry me home. Swing

cha - ri - ot, com-ing for to car-ry me home. Swing

sim.

49
sweet cha - ri - ot coming for oh
low, sweet cha - ri - ot, com-ing for to car-ry me
low, sweet cha - ri - ot, com-ing for to car-ry me
low, sweet cha - ri - ot, com-ing for to car-ry me
low, sweet cha - ri - ot, com-ing for to car-ry me
sim.
52
car-ry me home car-ry me home
home, com-ing for to car-ry me home,
home, com-ing for to car-ry me home,
home, com-ing for to car-ry me home,
home, com-ing for to car-ry me home,

rit.
55
p
com - ing for to car - ry me home.
com - ing for to car - ry me home.
com - ing for to car - ry me home.
com - ing for to car - ry me home.
com - ing for to car - ry me home.

Bless The Lord

Traditional
Arranged by Chris Norton & Leroy Johnson

8
all that is with - in me bless His ho - - - - - -
all that is with - in me bless His ho - - -
all that is with - in me bless His ho - - - - - -
all that is with - in me bless His ho - - - - -
11
- ly name.
- ly name.
- ly name.
- ly name.

14
più f
Bless the Lord, O my soul, and all that is with-
Bless the Lord, O my soul, and all that is with-
Bless the Lord, O my soul, and all that is with-
Bless the Lord, O my soul, and all that is with-
più f
17
in me bless His ho - - - - - - - ly
in me bless His ho - - - - - - ly
in me bless His ho - - - - - - - ly
in me bless His ho - - - - - - - ly

20

name.

name.

name.

name.

22

mp

He has done great things for me,

cresc.

He has done great

mp

He has done great things for me,

cresc.

He has done great

mp

He has done great things for me,

cresc.

He has done great

mp

He has done great things for me,

cresc.

He has done great

mp

sim.

cresc.

25
f
mp
things for me, He has done great things, Bless His
28
ho - ly name.
mf

30
mp
cresc.
He has done great things for me, He has done great
He has done great things for me, He has done great
He has done great things for me, He has done great
He has done great things for me, He has done great
sim.
33
f
mp
things for me, He has done great things, Bless His
things for me, He has done great things, Bless His
things for me, He has done great things, Bless His
things for me, He has done great things, Bless His

36
ho - ly name.
ho ly name.
ho - ly name.
ho - ly name.
38
mf
Bless the Lord, O my soul, and
Bless the Lord, O my soul, and
Bless the Lord, O my soul, and
Bless the Lord, O my soul, and

40
all that is with - in me bless His ho - - - - - -
all that is with - in me bless His ho - - - -
all that is with - in me bless His ho - - - - - -
all that is with - in me bless His ho - - - -
43
- ly name.
- ly name.
- ly name.
- ly name.
mf

46
più f
Bless the Lord, O my soul, and all that is with-
più f
Bless the Lord, O my soul, and all that is with-
più f
Bless the Lord, O my soul, and all that is with-
più f
Bless the Lord, O my soul, and all that is with-
più f
49
in me bless His ho - - - - - -
in me bless His ho - - -
in me bless His ho - - - - - -
in me bless His ho -

51

p

- ly name, Bless His

- ly name, Bless His

- ly name, Bless His

- ly name, Bless His

p

54

poco rit. . . . .

ho - - - - - ly name.

ho - - - - - ly name.

ho - - - - - ly name.

ho - - - - - ly name.

poco rit. . . . .

Go Tell It On The Mountain

Traditional
Arranged by Chris Norton & Leroy Johnson

8
moun - tain, ov - er the hills and ev - ery - where.
moun - tain, ov - er the hills and ev - ery - where.
moun - tain, ov - er the hills and ev - ery - where.
moun - tain, ov - er the hills and ev - ery - where.
11
Go tell it on the moun - tain that Je - sus Christ is born.
Go tell it on the moun - tain that Je - sus Christ is born.
Go tell it on the moun - tain that Je - sus Christ is born.
Go tell it on the moun tain that Je - sus Christ is born.

Soprano solo (freely)
14
mf
Won't you tell it on the moun - tain,
ov-er the hills,
Go tell it on the moun - tain,
Go tell it on the moun - tain,
Go tell it on the moun - tain,
Go tell it on the moun tain,
17
and ev - ery - where
ov - er the hills and ev - ery - where. Go tell it on the
ov - er the hills and ev - ery - where. Go tell it on the
ov - er the hills and ev - ery - where. Go tell it on the
ov - er the hills and ev - ery - where. Go tell it on the

20
Je - sus Christ,_ Je - sus Christ_ is born._
moun - tain that Je - sus Christ_ is born._
moun - tain that Je - sus Christ_ is born._
moun - tain that Je - sus Christ_ is born._
moun - tain that Je - sus Christ is born._
23
mp
When I was_ a seek - er,_ I sought both night and day._
mp
27
I asked the Lord to help_ me_ and He showed me the

31
way. Hey
ov - er the hills,
mf
Go tell it on the moun - tain,
mf
Go tell it on the moun - tain,
mf
Go tell it on the moun - tain,
mf
Go tell it on the moun - tain,
mf
34
and ev - ery - where
ov - er the hills and ev - ery - where. Go tell it on the
ov - er the hills and ev - ery - where. Go tell it on the
ov - er the hills and ev - ery - where. Go tell it on the
ov - er the hills and ev - ery - where. Go tell it on the

37
tell it on the moun - tain
woh,
moun - tain that Je - sus Christ is born.
moun - tain that Je - sus Christ is born.
moun - tain that Je - sus Christ is born.
moun - tain that Je - sus Christ is born.
40
go ov - er the hills and ev - ery-
Go tell it on the moun - tain, ov - er the hills and
Go tell it on the moun - tain, ov - er the hills and
Go tell it on the moun - tain, ov - er the hills and
Go tell it on the moun - tain, ov - er the hills and

43
where oh, go
tell 'em that Je - sus Christ
ev - ery - where.
Go tell it on the moun - tain that
46
Je - sus is born
Je - sus Christ is born, that

48
f
Oh
fp
Je - sus Christ is born, that
Je - sus Christ is born, that
Je - sus Christ is born, that
Je - sus Christ is born, that
50
Oh.
Je - sus Christ is born.
Je - sus Christ is born.
Je - sus Christ is born.
Je - sus Christ is born.
dim.
p